MODERN
Princess Tales

Sleeping Beauty

Beauty

Cinderella

Little Mermaid

Snow White

- classics retold to inspire -

by Zoe Rhodes

A special thanks to the women in my
family who showed me their strength.

ZR

First edition published by Fleur Publishing, Inc.

All inquiries should be addressed to:
Fleur Publishing, Inc.
4 Embarcadero Center, 14th Floor
San Francisco, CA 94111
(415) 766-3512
contact@fleurpublishing.com

Library of Congress Catalog Card Number pending
ISBN 978-1-9461-6701-9

Illustrations by Christina "Smudge" Hanson
Cover Art by Gustavo Gutierrez
Coloring by Maria Leung

Date of Manufacture: December 2016

PRINTED IN THE U.S.A.

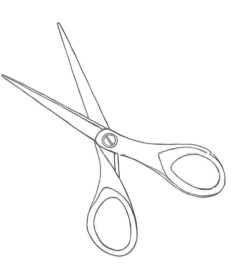

Table of Contents

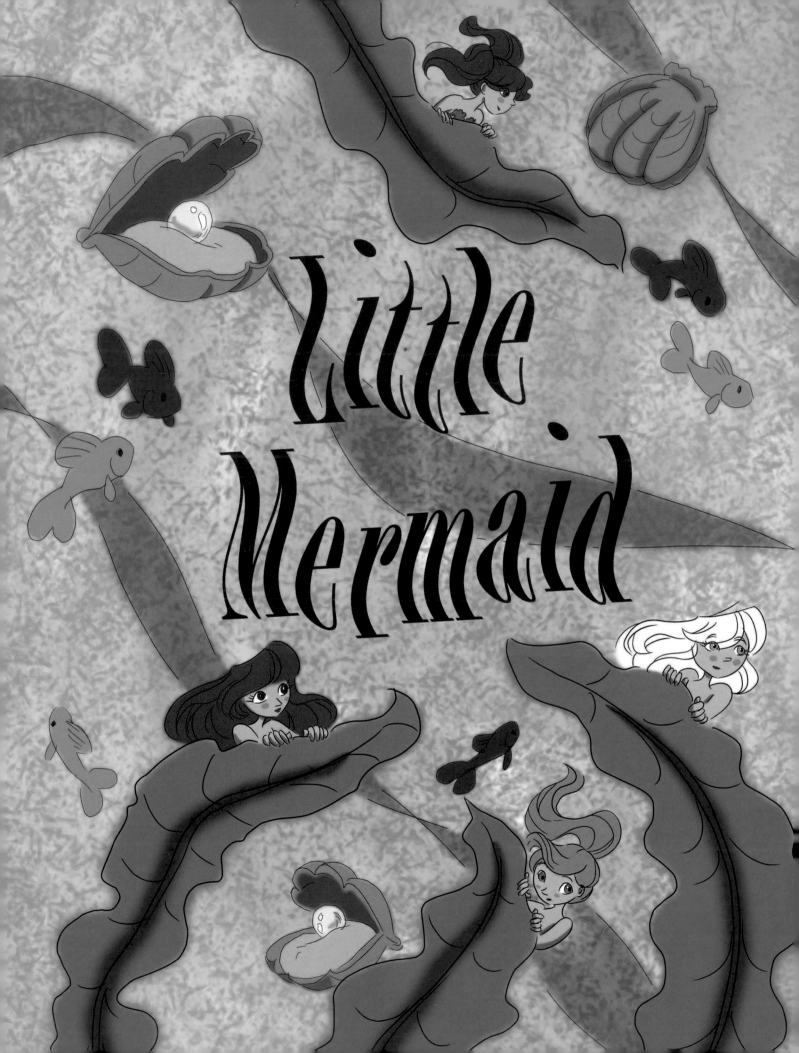

Little Mermaid

Once upon a time in a kingdom far, far away, there was a princess who lived deep under the sea. Her kingdom was colorful and busy with fish and merfolk swimming around. The palace was light with dark windows and everything in the kingdom was made of pure gold.

Surrounding the palace, little children played in the flower bushes as their parents worked. The princess's father ruled the entire ocean, as far as the waves could travel. She had five beautiful sisters. Although she was not the youngest, she was the smallest of her siblings. Her sisters called her Little Mermaid.

Every night, the sisters swam to the top of the sea, singing sweet, charming songs to the passing sailors. Little Mermaid was endlessly fascinated by humans and land. While all of her sisters cherished pearls and seashells from under the sea, Little Mermaid was more interested in treasures found in sunken ships, such as forks, pens, glasses, and shoes. Little Mermaid also adored how the town's lights glittered on the shore, like stars twinkling in the sky.

One night, Little Mermaid decided to visit the surface without her sisters. As she rose, she caught sight of a large ship full of singing and dancing people. She was so curious that she peeked through one of the portholes where she saw a handsome prince celebrating his birthday. He had big dark eyes and the most inviting smile Little Mermaid had ever seen. As she watched him greet people and talk with his friends, she began to fall in love.

2

Suddenly a storm broke out, the sky rumbled and the sea moved furiously. The ship bounced over giant, fierce waves until it could no longer stand. As the ship capsized, Little Mermaid saw the prince go overboard. She swam with all her might and brought the prince, who seemed to be dead, back to shore. She sat with him on the beach for hours, singing enchanting melodies, and hoping he would wake up.

At sunrise, Little Mermaid dove back into the sea and continued to watch the prince from a rock off shore. Soon, a few people found the prince and he woke up. Little Mermaid was so happy that she could not stop thinking about him after she returned home.

3

Three days later, Little Mermaid prepared
to celebrate her eighteenth birthday. As
was the custom, each princess was granted one
wish from the Sea Fairy on her eighteenth birthday.
To everyone's surprise, Little Mermaid wished for legs. The Sea
Fairy cautioned Little Mermaid that to receive legs, she would also have to give up her
voice. She explained that mermaids with legs are the best dancers on land because
they glide across the floor, as if they were in the ocean, but they do not have voices.
Little Mermaid listened to the Sea Fairy's words, but still chose the gift of legs.

When Little Mermaid reached shore and the townspeople saw her glorious movements, they dressed her in a nice gown and brought her to the palace. The prince instantly fell in love with Little Mermaid.

Even though she could not speak, the prince was mesmerized by her big green eyes and her beautiful smile. There was only one problem: the king and queen had already arranged for the prince to marry a princess from another kingdom in one year's time. The prince did not want to lose Little Mermaid, so he became close friends with the mysterious dancing beauty.

A year passed, and Little Mermaid and the prince became inseparable. Little Mermaid also attended university where she loved learning about science. Little Mermaid had seen her kingdom troubled by pollution and garbage. She was determined to use science to help her family's home.

On the day of her youngest sister's eighteenth birthday, Little Mermaid took a small boat out to sea and looked down at the joyous celebration in the depths of the ocean. She was sad and heartbroken because the prince would soon marry the other princess. She began to sing songs in her head, when suddenly she heard her voice singing out loud! Just then her sisters rose to the surface and told Little Mermaid that their youngest sister's one birthday wish was for Little Mermaid's voice to return. Her sisters missed her very much, but they wanted her to be happy on land and live her dreams. Little Mermaid jumped into the water and gave each of her sisters big hugs.

When Little Mermaid returned to the palace, she told a story and sang a song. The prince recognized her voice and knew she was the young girl who had saved him from the shipwreck. The prince immediately told his parents that Little Mermaid had saved his life and he was deeply in love with her. Seeing their son's joy, the king and queen blessed the young couple. The following year, Little Mermaid and the prince were married on a large ship with huge portholes, so her family could also enjoy the celebration.

After the wedding, Little Mermaid continued studying science. She captivated her professors with her vast knowledge of the ocean.

She worked hard to figure out scientific explanations for the wonders that lie deep in the glorious waters. After graduation, Little Mermaid became the first marine biologist in all the land. She won several awards and was known as one of the greatest scientists who ever lived because of her many discoveries that helped clean her dad's sea. And they all lived happily ever after.

9

Sleeping Beauty

Once upon a time in a land far, far away, there lived a king, a queen, and a newborn princess. When the princess was born, the king and queen held a royal ceremony and invited all the fairies in the kingdom to bless their innocent daughter.

The magical fairies were small, sweet and more powerful than a tornado. The first four fairies gave the princess the gifts of beauty, wit, grace and creativity. In exchange for their favors, the king and queen presented each of the fairies with spectacular, shimmering gold wands.

Suddenly, before the fifth fairy could bless the princess, an estranged old fairy who had disappeared from the kingdom long ago, arrived at the ceremony. The king and queen were surprised by her sudden appearance, and realized that they had not made a gold wand for her. The old fairy's face turned red with anger and her eyes bulged from her head. In a loud, shrieking voice, she cast a spell saying, "The princess will prick her finger on a needle and die!" The queen gasped and broke into tears.

The youngest fairy still had not blessed the princess, but she could not undo the curse. Instead, the sassy, clever fairy said, "The princess will not die when she pricks her finger; she will fall into a deep sleep for one hundred years and will only wake up when kissed by a prince." From that day on, needles were banished from the kingdom.

Eighteen years later, the princess went to college. While doing a research project, she visited a neighboring kingdom where needles were used.

The princess had never travelled to other kingdoms, so she was as curious as a baby owl about every new thing she saw. When seeing a sewing machine for the first time, the princess was thrilled and asked if she could try it. Within seconds of touching the sewing machine, the princess pricked her finger on the needle and fell to the ground. The seamstress frantically called the king and queen, and they carried the princess back to their palace.

They called her Sleeping Beauty because she radiated pure beauty even while she lay asleep. Since no person alive would be able to protect Sleeping Beauty for one hundred years, the youngest fairy again cast a spell making everyone in the palace freeze in time and space until Sleeping Beauty awoke. The fairy also made enchanted trees grow around the palace. The trees bent and burrowed into one another, creating a barrier as strong as steel, so no one could enter the palace.

15

One hundred years later, a young prince happened to be riding through what had become the deep forest when he saw the tip of the castle above the treetops. He stopped and asked his men, "What lies there?" One man stood and said in a husky voice, "Families of child-eating ogres live there, Your Highness." But the prince knew that ogres did not exist. A second man said in a low whisper, "My father told me that is where witches go to cast spells, Your Highness." But the prince did not believe this story either. Then an old man who was walking by offered, "Well, Your Highness, my grandfather told me that the most beautiful princess in the world lies asleep in that castle only to be awakened by the kiss of a prince." The prince tied up his horse and walked into the forest. The trees creaked as they untwisted and straightened to make a path for him. He looked back and saw the trees rearrange themselves again, so that his men could not follow.

The prince entered the palace and found
Sleeping Beauty lying on her gold-encrusted bed.
She was the most gorgeous young lady he had ever
seen and he instantly fell in love. When he kissed her
forehead, she opened her eyes and melted into his
kind, gentle smile. They talked for hours as if they had
known each other forever.

That evening, the prince invited Sleeping Beauty's parents to his palace and told them, along with his own parents, that he would marry Sleeping Beauty. Both sets of parents were overjoyed and made spectacular plans for the wedding. They ordered the finest food, decorations, entertainment, and gowns the land had ever seen. The invitations were sewn with silk thread and spun gold.

Meanwhile, Sleeping Beauty arose with an awful pain in her neck. She was determined to figure out a solution to this problem. The next morning, in a spark of creativity, she sketched a pillow design on a piece of paper to comfort her neck and showed it to a craftsman. Sleeping Beauty's pillow design worked so well that she started a company named SB Pillows that is still the largest and most successful business in the kingdom. Sleeping Beauty was the founder and C.E.O. of SB Pillows. She provided jobs to everyone who had been frozen in time, and more.

And they all lived happily ever after.

Cinderella

Once upon a time in a land far, far away, there was a young girl who was called Cinderella. Her father was a travelling businessman and her mother was a sweet soul who adored Cinderella. Cinderella and her mother loved running through the flowers in the meadow behind their house.

They would sit on the soft, silky grass and Cinderella's mother would teach her how to make flower necklaces out of the periwinkle blue and cotton-candy pink flowers that surrounded them.

When Cinderella was quite young, her mother became terribly ill and died. She spent several hours each day visiting her mother's grave in the meadow. Cinderella watched the tree limbs dance in the wind and knew that everything was alive. Her mother's spirit remained in the meadow.

A year later, Cinderella's father married a woman with two daughters and a broken heart. Her stepmother and stepsisters bullied Cinderella while her father was away on business. They made her work day and night, scrubbing floors, washing dishes, and cleaning the fireplace. The ashes and dirt soiled Cinderella's skin and clothes, but the sparkle remained in her eyes. While Cinderella's stepmother and stepsisters shopped for fantastic, fabulous fabrics to make lovely gowns, Cinderella went to the meadow and daydreamed about having her own beautiful dresses.

Occasionally, Cinderella mysteriously stumbled upon pieces of luxurious silk and brilliant jewels throughout the meadow. She carefully hid these treasures in a box under her bed where her stepmother and stepsisters could not find them.

That winter, the king organized a ball and invited all of the young women in the land so that his son, the young prince, could find a wife. The snotty stepsisters were beyond excited. They spent many days shopping for custom designer dresses, and primping their hair, skin, and nails, in the hopes that one of them would be the chosen maiden. But their hearts remained as cold and harsh as a winter blizzard. The stepmother did not even allow Cinderella to buy a dress for the ball. She was forced to continue working day and night in dirty rags.

One day, when Cinderella was sitting in the meadow, she had an idea. She remembered the silk fabrics and jewels she had saved and started to imagine a flowing gown. Cinderella had never made a ball gown, but she was determined to try.

That night, in a dream, she pictured herself wearing the most magnificent ball gown she had ever seen. She woke up in the middle of the night and sketched the dress. Each night, while everyone was sleeping, Cinderella spent hours cutting, stitching and creating her gown.

On the day of the ball, Cinderella tried on her gown and it fit like sprinkles on ice cream.

But the dress was not enough.
Cinderella still did not have shoes to wear,
and her stepmother left her a long list of
chores that could never be finished before
the ball. When her stepsisters left for the ball,
Cinderella went out to the meadow and cried.

Through her foggy tears, Cinderella suddenly saw two shimmering golden slippers next to her under the tree. She put her dress back on, and the slippers slid onto her feet like a charm. At the same moment, gold ribbons and diamonds fell perfectly from above onto Cinderella's hair and dress. A strong breeze blew over Cinderella, making her as fresh as pure water flowing in a steam, and she was ready to go. "The chores can wait," she thought as she happily ran off to the ball.

Cinderella was so stunningly gorgeous that she instantly captured the prince's attention. She was the only young lady he wanted to talk with the entire evening.

Dancing with the prince felt like floating on air. Cinderella hadn't been that joyful since she was a child, running through the flowers with her mother. At the end of the night, when the prince asked Cinderella where she lived, she ran off, accidently leaving a golden slipper on the stairs as she vanished into the night. The prince tried to follow her, but he could only see the neighborhood she entered.

The next day, the prince visited all the houses in her neighborhood, in order to find Cinderella. When he arrived at her house, her father called to Cinderella and she came out wearing rags covered in ashes. But as soon as Cinderella lifted her head, the prince saw the same sparkle in her eyes that he fell in love with at the ball and said, "This is my bride." He put the golden slipper on her foot and it slid on with ease. Her stepsisters couldn't believe it. Cinderella was beyond happy and agreed to marry the prince.

Cinderella Designs

Visions of fabrics in beautiful forms continued to appear in Cinderella's dreams and she rose each dawn to create unique designs. Cinderella became the kingdom's most famous fashion designer. Her dresses were sought after around the globe. She hired a team of young women, many of whom had also been treated unfairly as children, and she taught them to design and create fashions as well. The ladies loved working for Cinderella Designs, where they enjoyed all the perks of the splendid castle. They were surrounded by lush fabrics, majestic jewels, and laughter.

And they all lived happily ever after.

Beauty and Beast

Once upon a time in a land far, far away, there was a young girl named Beauty.

Her father was a successful businessman and her family had everything they desired. Beauty and her five brothers and sisters lived in a large home in town. Their comfortable, cinnamon-scented house sat in the main square, surrounded by fancy, frolicking people. But one day, her father lost their fortune and they were forced to move to a small house, far from town. Beauty's siblings complained about their new house, but Beauty remained happy. Her books transported Beauty on exciting journeys, so she was not bothered by her surroundings.

One day, Beauty's father had to travel far for a business trip. He asked all of his children what they wanted from his travels. Each child gave him a long list of requests, but Beauty only asked for one thing – a rose. She explained that roses are special because they create a lingering scent of flowery delight.

On his way home from the business trip, Beauty's father was caught in a terrible snowstorm and his car stalled on the road. Just when he thought the cold would kill him, he saw a warm, glowing castle in the distance.

Beauty's father walked up the pathway and was greeted by a gruesome beast. He desperately needed help and, although the beast was ugly, the beast fed him and gave him a safe place to rest. The next day, as Beauty's father was leaving, he picked a rose from the garden. The beast rushed out in a rage and said, "How dare you steal from me after I hosted you!" Beauty's father trembled with fear. In a stuttering voice, Beauty's father explained his misfortune and that he was hoping to at least bring a rose to Beauty. The beast agreed to let him go, under one condition: Beauty's father had to bring Beauty back within one week to stay at the beast's castle for an entire month.

When Beauty's father arrived home, he told the children about his treacherous travels and his encounter with the beast. After one week, Beauty said to her father, "It is time to go. We must keep your promise to the beast who saved your life." Beauty was frightened, but she was also brave and strong. She brought only a few things with her, including her books. She knew that no matter where she went, her books would be like friends and keep her company.

When Beauty arrived at the castle, she was surrounded by a warm, sweet feeling. The beast was terrifying, but kind. Beauty spent her days at the castle exploring all the rooms, including her favorite room, the library. The bookshelves were packed to the ceiling with books of all shapes and sizes. Her favorite thing to do was bring a ladder to different parts of the library and find books on the top shelves that few people had read. She would wrap herself in pillows on the soft suede sofa and read until her eyes could read no more. Each evening at dinner, the beast talked with Beauty. His voice was scratchy and scary, but his words were gentle. The more they talked, the more Beauty enjoyed life at the castle.

At night in Beauty's dreams, a handsome prince often appeared and asked her to save him. He also warned Beauty that she should not be deceived by appearances. Beauty recognized the prince from the paintings on the walls of the castle. She thought that maybe the beast was holding the prince prisoner somewhere in the castle.

Beauty began to miss her family and asked the beast if she could visit home. He agreed, but told her that if she did not return within one month, he would die. When Beauty arrived home, her siblings jumped with joy. They surrounded Beauty and listened as she told them about the beast and his marvelous castle. Beauty told them that she loved everything about the beast, except for his frightening looks. After Beauty had been home for one month, she had a dream that the beast was dying.

The next day, Beauty rushed back to the castle concerned for the beast's life. She found the beast dying in the garden. Tears streamed down her face, and with every breath she took, her heart felt as though it was breaking into a million little pieces. With one of his last breaths, the beast asked, "Beauty, will you marry me?"

Beauty answered, "Yes, yes, I will!" At that moment, fireworks erupted in the sky and the beast turned into the handsome prince from her dreams. The prince explained that a curse had been cast upon him that only true love could break. Beauty and the prince were soon married in a gorgeous wedding, overflowing with roses.

Beauty Communications
Beauty Publishing
Beauty Productions

After the wedding, Beauty decided to write a book about her story with the beast. She learned it was important to look beyond the surface, and she wanted to share this with the world. The book became a bestseller and was made into a movie. Beauty then began writing about other people's meaningful stories. As a result of her success, Beauty started a production company that owned all types of media, including television and radio stations, movie studios and Internet channels. Beauty was the first media mogul in the kingdom. Everyone who met Beauty loved her positivity and admired her amazing productions.

And they all lived happily ever after.

Once upon a time in a land far, far away, there lived a little girl named Snow White. Her skin was as white as snow and her hair was as black as night. Snow White had two happy homes. She lived with her father half of the year and with her mother the other half. Snow White was kind to everyone and loved taking care of the children in her neighborhood.

The queen in Snow White's kingdom was insecure and vain. Each day, the queen looked into her magical mirror and said, "Mirror on the wall, who is the prettiest of them all?" and the mirror replied, "You are the most beautiful in the kingdom." One day, however, on Snow White's sixteenth birthday, the mirror replied, "You, My Queen, are pretty, but Snow White is the most beautiful in the kingdom." The queen was enraged. She could not bear to hear of anyone more beautiful than herself.

In her fury, the queen called
a huntsman and ordered him to take
Snow White deep into the dark woods
outside of the kingdom walls. When the
huntsman left Snow White alone in the
twisted tangle of treacherous woods,
she was terrified and didn't know which
way to run. Snow White ran and ran
until she found a small cabin.

When she knocked on the door, no one answered so she opened the door and walked in. The house seemed to be made for children, with miniature furniture and tiny clothes. As Snow White wandered through the house, she came across a little bedroom with neatly made beds. A marvelous blue vase decorated the dresser. The wooden walls were sprinkled with bright yellow and green paintings of the forest.

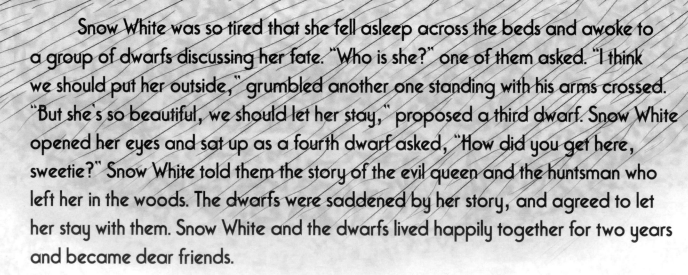

Snow White was so tired that she fell asleep across the beds and awoke to a group of dwarfs discussing her fate. "Who is she?" one of them asked. "I think we should put her outside," grumbled another one standing with his arms crossed. "But she's so beautiful, we should let her stay," proposed a third dwarf. Snow White opened her eyes and sat up as a fourth dwarf asked, "How did you get here, sweetie?" Snow White told them the story of the evil queen and the huntsman who left her in the woods. The dwarfs were saddened by her story, and agreed to let her stay with them. Snow White and the dwarfs lived happily together for two years and became dear friends.

One day, Snow White was gathering berries and accidentally crossed the boundary into her old kingdom.

That day, when the queen spoke to her mirror, the mirror replied, "You, My Queen, are pretty, but Snow White is still the most beautiful person in the kingdom."

The queen was frantic and thought of a plan to poison Snow White. She went deep into the forest, disguised as an old woman. She approached Snow White while she was gathering berries and offered her a crisp, delicious, red apple that was secretly poisoned. Snow White was so hungry from gathering food all day that she couldn't resist.

As soon as Snow White took a bite, she fell to the ground. After the dwarfs came home, they searched for Snow White for hours in the forest. The dwarfs were devastated to find her on the ground. They placed Snow White in an elegant glass case so her beauty could be seen from all sides. At that moment, a young prince from a neighboring kingdom rode by on his horse.

He thought Snow White was so magnificent that he stopped and begged the dwarfs, "Let me take her to my kingdom and I promise to honor her." The dwarfs knew that the prince was a kind man and would protect Snow White. However, just as the prince began the journey back to his kingdom, one of his men carrying the case tripped on a rock. The jolt caused the piece of poisonous apple, still stuck in Snow White's throat, to fly out and she slowly began to wake up.

When they arrived at the castle, the prince told Snow White that he had fallen in love with her. At first, Snow White was skeptical of the prince and asked to go back to the cabin in the woods, with the dwarfs. The prince agreed, and he visited Snow White in the forest for many months.

Over time, she began to fall for his loving eyes, caring smile and kind heart. Snow White finally agreed to marry the prince in the most splendid wedding the land had ever seen. The wedding cake, decorated with diamonds and rubies, was taller than three dwarfs high. Everyone in the kingdom, including the dwarfs, was invited. Meanwhile, the queen's jealousy spoiled her heart and she became ugly.

Snow White's mother and father visited her new kingdom often, but she was sad that the dwarfs didn't visit her so much.

When the dwarfs came to her wedding, she noticed it was hard for them because the town wasn't built for little people. She felt bad for her friends and wanted to make a change.

Little People of the Kingdom

Snow White found the smartest people in the kingdom, including some of the dwarfs, to help her start a non-profit organization. They created a group called Little People of the Kingdom to spread awareness about dwarfs. They worked with the town's people in order to make the dwarfs more comfortable. The dwarfs were delighted and visited Snow White often.

And they all lived happily ever after.

51